KAREN ANN SMYTHE
Amazing Adventures of
Fredrick The Butterfly
Plus Karen & Malibu Kool Kat !
PEACE
LOVE

To my Most Loving Grandparents,
Agnes "Nunnie" Kearns Smythe and Victor David Smythe,
who were always there for me, during my Childhood.

Julia Smythe Turner and Veronica Smythe Turner.
I Honestly Love both of my daughters with all my
whole being!

My Belated Husband, Peter Ezra Turner, we Loved each
other so much, we were a Great Team too!

My Very Loving Parents
Maryann Theresa McMahon Hopkins Smythe
David Lawrence Smythe Sr.

My Three Caring Brothers
David Lawrence Smythe Jr.
Thomas William Smythe
Special Love to my Brother James Michael Smythe

My Extra Special Mother-In-Law
Joyce Turner Hilkevitch

My two Sisters-In-Law and two Brothers-In-Law
"Who were always there for my daughters and myself during
my Adulthood," Susan Turner Jones, Janis Pretzlav,
David Turner, David Thomson Jones

Virginia Hurley Olsen

My Dear Friends Anna and Morris Dalva

Thank you to the town of Summit, New Jersey for being such
a safe and beautiful environment to grow up in!

ABOUT ME

This is what happened. This is it! I was the first girl born into our family in 102 years! Well, that made me feel special from the beginning. As I grew older, I realized that Father was a successful businessman and entrepreneur. More than once he would lean toward me and say, "Karen, you must learn the value of a dollar, do not spend money you don't have." In other words, he was telling me not to buy foolish things and never buy anything on credit if you can help it. I would nod in agreement, appreciating the fact he was trying to teach me principles that made him such a huge success.

During family dinner, Dad and I would often have nice, interesting, informative conversations about people and also about business deals he had working. He was very open to discuss business matters with me and often ask my opinion. As mentioned, he encouraged me to be wise with finances and have good judgement about money. I grew up actually understanding interest rates and stock prices. I also learned that "giving back" was not an option; it was a requirement that our family help others less fortunate. So, I also heard this a thousand times, "To whom much is given, much is required." It was from the Bible I think. Giving was just in our DNA and it just so happened to be one of the most enjoyable things I would do for the rest of my life.

There were other tidbits of advise offered from both Mom and Dad which will stay with me for a lifetime, I'm sure:

"Stay relaxed and free from tension as much as possible." "Keep the Faith" "Say your prayers – God will listen and help you." "Do not make a decision when you are angry. Cool down, take a walk around the block, or sleep on it." "Be kind to others." "Words mean a lot." "Stay safe - know enough to leave or get

Plaque on the front of my Grandparent's home that my Great, Great Grandfather built! The Smythe "Homestead."

out of a dangerous situation – always locate the nearest exit door." "Don't be afraid to take a risk – you can't stay in your shell like a turtle. Stick your head out, look around - go out and about. Enjoy yourself!" One of my favorites: "Keep a sense of humor." We did that one well. Laughing was big in my family. If you looked closer at our family you would also see that I was raised to eat fresh, healthy food, but not too much. We also knew the importance of plenty of exercise.

Through Father's hard work and creative ideas we came to be a somewhat wealthy family and for the first few years of my life, we lived next to my Grandparents whom I love very much. So, you can

Plaque on the side of the Smythe "Homestead."

understand why I was very sad when we had to move a little further away even though we remained in the same town of Summit. Dad had built a big house only two miles from my Grandparents' home, but, to me it seemed like we moved a hundred miles away.

My Grandparents were so special and gave a lot of love! At Christmas time I received lots of presents; the gifts from my Grandparents mostly came from the "five and dime" store. They would be wrapped in sparkly white paper with ribbon that you could curl at the ends using the the inside edge of the scissors. Usually inside the perfectly wrapped packages would be simple gifts like a pad of paper, a pen, a mirror, a hairbrush, a game of some sort. Also, every year we each received a handmade pair of slippers from my Grandmother.

A little history further back: My Great Grandfather owned quite a bit of land in Summit, including the well-traveled Blackburn Road, which he donated back to the city as a gift. He also established the Summit newspaper, The Summit Herald, and even owned a stone quarry in town. His Father, my Great-Great Grandfather, had been a doctor who established the prestigious Summit Health Dept. I am a blood relative of William Brewster who came over on the Mayflower and is in the History books.

Although I missed my Grandparents greatly I learned to love our new home and neighborhood. There was zero crime so we could play outside until dark and take walks even at night and feel safe. The neighbors were caring and welcoming. It wasn't long before I was helping the neighbors by raking leaves, shoveling snow in the winter, carrying groceries for them, babysitting, and watching their homes when they were away. They did the same for us, too. The neighbor kids and I played checkers, had tea parties, jumped rope in the backyard. We grew a vegetable garden, too, and made jelly from my very special grapevine and we always loved to make rhubarb soup and salads from the family garden!

Like most kids, I had a favorite secret place. Mine was the huge grapevine field across from my Grandparents' home. I had a place to sit and relax and think about what I wanted to be and do when I grew up. It was there I began to discover my spiritual self, my "Holy" self and realize there truly is something magnificent going on that makes everything okay; something that guides you to be good. Before leaving my secret place, I often filled a basket with grapes to bring home for Mom and Grandmother.

I loved to walk so countless times I would walk down to sit along a brook nearby, listening to it babble as I watched the pollywogs swim by. I also loved listening to the rain that would sometimes send me running home. Did you know that each raindrop has a different look, a different feeling; a different sound, a beat and a tune? Like each snowflake, a raindrop is intricately designed.

Holidays were special times of parties and gift-giving between families. My Father, who was extremely patriotic, loved the fact that all the neighbors proudly displayed the American flag on the 4th of July and the entire neighborhood made sure to visit one or all of the backyard BBQ's in progress.

"Never take your freedom for granted, young lady," Father would say, and I didn't. I was grateful for the blessings of being born an American! We all displayed our American flags through out the year. Plus, we cheered for each other (and other countries) to be well and do well! Actually, I grew up wanting to see and hear and help support others doing well! Cheers!

When I look into the mirror, I like myself! I love to practice cheerleading in front of the mirror. I have green-eyes with chestnut-colored hair that grows just past my shoulders. During summer months a few freckles arrive on my nose and my skin turns toasty-brown from hours of swimming and playing on the beach. My body is changing everyday it seems and I am still getting used to the new me.

I'm a tomboy at heart. I have climbed to the top of every tree on our property and the neighbor boys don't challenge me to a foot race anymore because I smoke them every time. I will try anything that has to do with nature; like fishing, camping, hiking and body-surfing in the ocean. I am definitely not a "girly-girl". However, I must admit, sometimes I love acting like a girly-girl! I have fun modeling and putting on plays in the summer. I get my friends together, then gather big pieces of driftwood to make a stage. Then, we sing and dance to "By the Sea". People actually stop and watch. That is so much fun.

It is such a beautiful world with so many wonderful, caring, beautiful, loving, kind and fun people to meet. Interesting isn't it? There are also so many things to see and do. And, people have just got to have love! I am determined to share this love and peace and kindness throughout my life! Even all the birdies go, "Chirp, chirp, chirp." The world is magnificent!

Lately, I have noticed this nagging feeling; a sense of something out there just beyond my reach calling to me. I know, sounds wacky, right? I tried to explain it to Mom this morning and she shrugged her shoulders and said, "Honey that is just adolescence happening to you. You'll be moody during these teen years and have lots of up and down, but try not to be too dramatic, Karen, it is normal and you are fine. You are discovering who you are, that is exciting for you!"

One night I just couldn't go to sleep, tossing and turning all night. Along with these new mysterious stirrings, I was missing my Grandparents so much. Around 3 a.m. I heard a fluttery sound and felt a gentle lick on my nose. I sat up in bed, realizing it was my two best friends, Fredrick, the butterfly and Malibu Kool Kat, my cat.

Are you freaked out, yet? Well, just wait, you haven't heard the half of it. I found Fredrick on the beach one summer when he was just about to be swept away by the waves. I rescued him, put him in a bucket and carried him home. We've been great friends ever since. Here's the thing. Fredrick is some sort of magical creature who never grows old and never changes. I love Fredrick so much and he has never been more than a glance away. Fredrick actually gives me great information! I always check with him in order to make right decisions.

As for Malibu Kool Kat – he was rescued after I heard that he was going to be abandoned in a house that sat deep into a forest area near where we live. When I found him he was dirty, hungry and scared, but ever since I brought him home, cleaned him up and gave him a lot of love, he has become the coolest cat ever – the "coolest of cool" cats. He is now a "therapy cat" who loves to visit the local bookstore where children read to him and pet him which makes him purr loudly. I even trained him to walk with a leash! Kool Kat is solid black with one patch of white fur, right over his heart. He really is cool and loved by everyone! Just like Fredrick, Kool Kat has a special way of communicating with me. He has an incredible vocabulary and provides sensational information, too.

So, on this particular night when I couldn't sleep, I sat up in bed and tried to tell my best friends what was going on with me. "I miss Grandfather and Grandmother so much tonight. Do you know that Grandpa let me read all the love letters he has ever sent my Grandma? They were so absolutely wonderful. But something else is going on, too. It's like I'm looking for something, but can't remember what it is," I told them, scratching my head and looking puzzled.

Fredrick hovered inches away from my freckled nose and said, "We will help you find whatever it is you are looking for."   Then he flapped his beautiful wings and flew a few feet to the north, then back to the east, the west, and finally to the south, signaling he was ready to go in any direction with me on my journey.

"Ah, thanks, dear Fredrick, but I wouldn't know where to start. I only know I have to find out what it is my heart is telling me to do. When I find out, I'll let you know," I said while reaching to scratch Kool Kat under his chin.

After a few seconds of loud purring, Kool Kat said, "Perhaps, dear Karen, it is time to lay aside your crown and find out what else is going on in the world!"

It's true that I had been treated like a princess, protected and sheltered from the outside world for most of my life. When at home I often donned a pretty, sparkling tiara I had kept since I was a little girl. I glanced over to the nightstand where it lay. I reached for it and held it in my hand, studying it for a moment before answering. "Yes, I think you are right. It's time." I opened the drawer of the nightstand and tossed the small crown inside. As I closed the drawer I felt the excitement of the new adventures to come. Once again my friends, Fredrick and Kool Kat, had calmed my fears and given me a new perspective to consider. I was ready.

I was asleep almost before my head hit the pillow with my new soft pillow case.

P.S. Before falling completely asleep, I was thinking and being thankful and grateful for all the good things that happen in life. For example, my Uncle John was an Air Force Pilot in World War 2. After leaving the Air Force he always had a little plane. I would go flying with him and he even let me fly the plane a little bit! Every summer my family would vacation on an island 6 miles out at sea (Long Beach Island, NJ). We would go fishing, crabbing and waterskiing. Sometimes when I went clamming I would sell the clams to the local fish market for a penny a piece. I also had a little sailboat that I learned to sail by myself + would take my friend. There are so many wonderful people in this world and beautiful places to see + visit + experience! We are all in the same situation! Floating and twirling around up in the sky on Planet Earth! Funny! You are here to enjoy yourself + help other people + the creatures that live here. An ant has a life + family + friends! Give Love and Receive Love!

The Adventures Begin: The "Peace Flags Project"

The next morning I woke refreshed and excited to begin the day. I dressed for school, brushed my hair then lifted it into a tight pony tail. I ran my fingers over Kool Kat's shiny coat and he stretched in an arch under my hand. "Have a great day, Kool Kat. You too, Fredrick," who was busy staring at the strawberries growing just outside my window.

"You too, Karen," Fredrick said, too mesmerized by the luscious looking strawberries to look in my direction.

I hurried downstairs for breakfast and overheard Father talking about something he had been reading in his morning newspaper. "This is so sad. There are families trying to get out of their own countries because of the threat of war and many risk their lives and their children's lives just trying to escape."

Mother agreed, "It is a shame when innocent victims, like children, are suffering because governments can't get along."

I listened intently as Father added, "And, those who stay are facing the worst possible conditions, even starvation."

Suddenly, the cinnamon toast I usually had for breakfast was not as delicious. I pushed my plate away and asked, "What can we do about it, Father?" wondering if this could be part of the new adventure awaiting me and Fredrick and Kool Kat.

He smiled gently. "Not much, I'm afraid. Our government is sending food, but it often ends up in the wrong hands and doesn't go to the people who need it most. It is just tragic." Then the subject was changed and the conversation went on, but my mind stayed focused on the countries under threat of war.

I excused myself, ran up to my room and rummaged through my closet until I found it; a rolled map of the world stuffed into one corner. I spread the map on top of my bed as Fredrick looked over my shoulder. I placed my finger on the country Father had mentioned. "There it is, the country having trouble; the one Father was talking about, Kalendestine. There are people living there who are afraid everyday. And, there are children who don't have enough food. That is terrible."

Malibu Kool Kat crept closer and plopped down on the map close to my finger. "There must be something someone can do," he said twisting his head almost completely around like cats can do.

Fredrick added, "What is the opposite of war?"

"Peace," Kool Kat and I answered at the very same time.

"That's it, Fredrick. The world needs peace and we have to deliver that message. Wait a minute, I think I know a way!" I went to my desk and pulled out a sheet of paper and a carton of colored pencils and went to work. When finished, I folded the picture and placed it in my backpack along with my school books. Cutting it close, I had just enough time to run downstairs, pick up my sack lunch and make it out the door in time to leave for school.

One of my favorite teachers at Summit High School is Miss Johnson, my first-period history teacher. She has curly light brown hair and brown eyes that twinkle when she smiles and a way of telling stories that make history so interesting. After class that day, I stayed after to ask her a question. "Miss Johnson, I have an idea I want to tell you about. Do you have a second?"

"Well, of course I do, Karen." She sat down at her desk and motioned for me to sit in the chair next to her. I began to explain that I wanted to take a message of peace and hope to countries at risk because of the threat of war.

"Yes, war is a terrible thing, Karen, but, honestly, I don't know what one person could do."

"Well, what about this?" Then, I pulled from my backpack the picture I had made that morning. I had drawn a large capitol "P" on a stick, signifying peace, with the names of many countries in the world written on it. The background was light blue.

"That is lovely, Karen, but I don't understand," she said kindly.

"I call it a peace flag."

"Yes, I see … a peace flag."

"Here's my idea, Miss Johnson. Maybe one flag wouldn't mean much, but what if we could get everyone in our history classes to create their own peace flag? Perhaps then, we could send them all to the leader of a country under the threat of war to show how very sad we are about what that is doing to their country and that we hope peace will come soon."

As students began to make their way into the class for the next period, I had Miss Johnson's full attention. "Hmmm … I tell you what, I will ask Principal Gregory for permission to do the project with my students. We'll call it 'The Peace Flags Project.' Do you like that?"

"Oh, yes, Miss Johnson, that's perfect." I couldn't keep from smiling the biggest smile and feeling so happy!

"May I keep your drawing to show Mr. Gregory?"

"Sure," I said, as I rose from the chair. I heard the bell ring for the next class as soon as I entered the hall, so I ran as fast as I could toward my 2nd period math class with Mr. Garrett. He was just closing the door to the classroom as I arrived out of breath. "Sorry, I'm late, Mr. Garrett. I was talking to Miss Johnson."

Second period was half over when the loud speaker came on with a squeak in the classroom. "Attention, Mr. Garrett: Karen Smythe is needed in the principal's office."

Mr. Garrett was working on a long division

problem on the chalkboard when the entire class went, "Oooohhh!" A chorus of snickers followed.

"Yes, thank you. I'll send her right away," Mr. Garrett said, then turned my way, "Miss Smythe, would you please take your books and report to the principal's office."

I could feel my face redden as all eyes turned to look at me. Billy Tunstall, who sat directly across from me whispered loudly, "What did you do, Smythe? Whatever it was, you're in trouble now. Hope you don't cry like a baby."

"Be quiet, Billy," I said as I gathered my books and backpack. It didn't even dawn on me that Miss Johnson could have talked to the principal about the project that quickly. I was nervous as I walked to the front of the school where the administrative offices were located.

Directly behind the school's check-in/check-out counter was Mr. Gregory's office. His door was wide open so when he saw me, he motioned me in. "Miss Smythe, Miss Johnson has told me about your "Peace Flags Project" and I agree that it is a wonderful idea. I have given Miss Johnson permission to ask her students to join you in creating the flags. We are very proud of you."

"Thanks, Mr. Gregory," I managed, trying to contain how happy I felt inside.

"You are free to return to class, we both just wanted to tell you that good ideas like yours are always welcome here at Summit High School. We all will be happy to help with the project in any way, we can. Thank you, Miss Smythe. Oh, and here's your peace flag picture."

Miss Johnson gave me a strong hug as we both stood to exit Mr. Gregory's office. I hurried back to class, took my seat, but couldn't stop smiling, much to Billy Tunstall's disappointment. He just kept staring at me.

That evening, I rushed home from school and flew upstairs to tell Fredrick and Kool Kat about the "Peace Flags Project". They were elated. "I feel it. This is new adventure coming for all of us," Fredrick said, "and I can't wait to see where it takes us."

That evening at dinner I shared my idea for the "Peace Flags Project" with my parents. I could tell both Mother and Father were very proud. "Why, Karen – that is a wonderful idea, dear. How did you ever come up with it?" Mother asked.

"I had a little help from friends," I said, glancing toward my bedroom upstairs. My parents had not yet learned about Fredrick and Kool Kat's special gifts of communication. Perhaps someday when the time was right they would love getting to know about Fredrick and Kool Kat's special powers, too.

That night getting ready for bed I thought about the innocent victims of conflicts between countries around the world, especially the children. I imagined they were calling for help. Just before I fell asleep, I whispered, "I hear you, I hear you."

KALENDESTINE – HERE WE COME!

You should have seen them! I couldn't have imagined all the great ideas everyone used to create the flags. There were 150 flags with all kinds of designs on them: rainbows, doves, trees, flowers, two fingers making the "peace" sign, hearts, smiley faces, animals, oceans, sunsets, mountains and on and on. They were beautiful! Everyone signed their flags and some of the students wrote special messages on the flags like, "Praying for Peace", "We are Thinking of You", "Choose Peace, Not War", "With Love – Your American Friends", "From the USA to U" and "Hoping War Ends Soon", and many others.

Miss Johnson came up with the idea to attach all the flags to a strong cord, so that when the cord was extended each flag could be seen. "You know, Karen, now it is time to decide where the flags will go and who will receive them. Since you started the project I think it is a good idea for you to discuss it with your parents then make a choice as to where the flags will be sent."

Following dinner that evening my parents and I discussed several countries experiencing the threat of war, including the small nation Dad read about in the newspaper, Kalendestine.

"I want our flags to go to Kalendestine," I said.

Imagine my surprise when Father said, "Do you know what would be truly wonderful, since it is your project? If you could go to Kalendestine and deliver the flags in person."

I gulped, not believing my ears. "Dad, really? You would let me go? That is awesome! Yea!"

"It would be the adventure of a lifetime and we would need to make sure you had protection; the world can be a dangerous place. What an opportunity to see that part of the world and deliver the flags yourself." I looked at Mother and she was nodding in agreement.

"Oh, yes, Dad. Wait … may I take two friends along?"

"Sure," he answered without hesitation. And, I knew just the two friends I would take along. "Boys!" I burst into my bedroom catching Kool Kat stalking his own shadow and Fredrick admiring himself in the dressing table mirror. "We are going to Kalendestine!"

THE TRIP OF A LIFETIME

The next few weeks were a blur of excitement. When I told Miss Johnson I had permission to make the trip to Kalendestine myself to deliver the flags, she was surprised. "Are you sure, Karen? That country is thousands of miles away. You will need to be extremely cautious. Part of the nation is experiencing unrest."

"I know, Miss Johnson, but, I am not going alone. I will have protection and two friends will make the trip with me." I didn't tell her that I would be making the trip with one special butterfly and a very smart and cool feline named Malibu Kool Kat.

My teachers made contact with a school in Kalendestine and the arrangements were made to present the flags to their student body. The language of the Kalendestine people was a mixture of French and Russian, so through a French interpreter they were able to explain the flags project and how the students at our school wanted to present the students there with our peace flags. The school officials were delighted. The date was set.

I went to the post office to get my passport photo made and my parents made sure I had all the necessary vaccination shots for the journey. I was growing more excited by the day. The town's newspaper reporter came to my school to take pictures and to interview me about the trip. He wanted to know all about the flag project and about my upcoming trip to Kalendestine. Before he left, the reporter told me to take lots of pictures to share with the newspaper when I returned home. It was only two weeks away! The next day the headline in our local paper read, "Young Girl on a Mission to Kalendestine with Peace Flags!"

In the days before departing for Kalendestine, I tried to practice a presentation speech in French, but I wasn't doing very well. "You know Karen, I believe you would do better just to deliver your speech in English. I'm sure there will be an interpreter present," Miss Johnson offered.

The day finally arrived for our departure. Father took us to the airport with Fredrick and Kool Kat tucked snugly inside a carrier. Before take-off I met Mr. Clark, a former policeman whom Father hired as my bodyguard.

"Now Karen, Mr. Clark will always be close by. You are to do exactly as he tells you. He will be looking out for your safety at all times. Understood?"

"Yes, Father. Hello, Mr. Clark."

"Hello, little Miss," the tall man in a black suit and black-rimmed sunglasses said. His voice was a deep, low whisper. "It will be an honor to travel with you." I wondered if Mr. Clark ever took off his sunglasses. Father and Mother gave me huge hugs and instructed me to call them as soon as I arrived in Kalendestine.

Young Girl on a Mission to Kalendestine with Peace Flags!
WORLD PEACE

We boarded the plane and settled in for the long trip overseas to Kalendestine. Mr. Clark sat in the row just behind me. I was hoping to see Mr. Clark smile once in a while on the trip, so I made it my goal to see that happen. I fell asleep listening to the drone of the plane's engines. It was a long flight. I knew that Fredrick and Kool Kat would be thrilled to be out of the carrier.

As soon as we landed, I retrieved the carrier from under the seat in front of me. The boys (Fredrick and Kool Kat) were griping about being pent up too long, "Come on, Karen – we need to stretch our legs," Kool Kat said.

"Not me – I need to stretch my wings," Fredrick chimed in. "Look, Kool Kat, you slept on my antennae! See – it's all crinkled," Fredrick added.

"All right, all right, you two. Your antennae will straighten out, Fredrick. You both need to stay in the carrier until we get through customs. Please try to act like a normal butterfly and cat, okay?"

"How humiliating," Fredrick said trying to stretch inside the carrier.

Mr. Clark helped with my bags as I toted the pet carrier to the line of people waiting for inspection by a rather stout woman who was the customs agent at the airport. She wore very thick glasses and held my passport nearly up to her nose to view my photo, then with a grunt, she stamped it, "Free to Travel."

Mr. Clark directed us to a jeep parked outside and

the hired driver came around to load the bags in the back. He tried to take the carrier from me that held Fredrick and Kool Kat, too. "Oh, no," I said, "this one stays with me."

He shrugged and gave me a hand up into the back seat of the jeep, while Mr. Clark sat in the front passenger seat. The driver, a dark-skinned young man with short, curly hair, took his seat at the wheel, then turned to me and said in broken English, "My name is Genespar. I take you to city of Corinza in Kalendestine. There are guerilla soldiers in mountains; enemies of Kalendestine. If we be stopped for any reason, I do all talking. Understand?"

Mr. Clark answered, "Understood."

Genespar looked at me and I shook my head up and down, "Yes, yes, sir," as a shiver ran up my spine. The warning sounded so ominous. It made me realize just how far I was from home.

Then, Genespar smiled a broad, happy smile, started the engine and began to whistle a happy tune as we left the airport parking lot. From there we would make the 250 mile trip into Kalendestine. As we traveled through the small towns and villages, we periodically stopped to wave the peace flags and say,"Hello" to the people of Kalendestine. They were wonderful and welcoming. Everyone loved the flags.

Kool Kat and Fredrick were having so much fun. Fredrick was flying in between and over and through the unfurled flags while Kool Kat scurried all around the people who enjoyed waving them in the streets and countryside. Even though we did not speak the same language there was a human understanding and agreement on one thing; we all want peace and love! We laughed and hugged so many friendly people and took many pictures. After all, laughter has no language.

Soon we left the towns behind and began to travel a winding road leading high into the mountains with dark, dense forests on either side. My eyes were heavy. It had been a long day, but I didn't want to sleep. There was no curb on our side of the road; one slight driving mistake, and Genespar could send us crashing to the valley floor below. I could not relax as the jeep rattled on, taking the sharp turns. I peered into the thick jungle bushes and trees that hung over the road.

A couple of hours into our trip just as I was beginning to doze off, Genespar, shouted, "Okay, remember I do talking!" I sat straight up as he slowed to a stop. Looking out the front window, I saw a large tarp-covered military truck blocking our way. A big, sober looking man with muscles everywhere approached the side of the car and Genespar rolled down the window. The man was dressed in khaki and green-colored camouflage and had an ugly-looking machine gun hanging from a shoulder strap. He said something gruffly to Genespar who in turn, said to Mr. Clark and me excitedly, "Passports … he wants see passports."

Mr. Clark carried mine for safe-keeping, so, he reached into his inside coat pocket, quickly whipped them out and passed them to the soldier. The soldier sneered as he looked at the photos in the passports and then glared at each of us to see if we matched the photos.

My heart was already beating fast when Genespar then said to Mr. Clark and me, "Out of car, hurry. Do what he say and make no sudden moves."

Mr. Clark came around to my side of the jeep and helped me out. With one hand I grabbed the handle of the carrier holding Fredrick and Kool Kat, then Mr. Clark held my other hand as we stood outside the car, waiting in the cool, crisp mountain air. I sat the carrier down and asked softly, "Mr. Clark, what does the angry man want?"

"I'm not sure, but it will be okay, Miss. I won't let anything or anyone hurt you."

Genespar walked to me and said, "I sorry, miss – soldier wants to know what is in there?" He was pointing at the carrier.

"Oh, It's just my cat and my pet butterfly," I answered nervously. Genespar delivered that news to the soldier who laughed then walked toward me himself. Suddenly, he grabbed the carrier, un-zipped the opening and shook it, laughing as he said something. His large hand went inside the carrier and Fredrick flew out while Kool Kat hissed at the intrusion, then ran out of the carrier to the edge of the forest where the trees met the road. Fredrick lighted on the top of the jeep. I was angry then.

"Hey," I said. "We've done nothing to you. We are on a peace mission. Why are you treating us like criminals?"

"Shhh, shhh, Miss … no, no, no," Genespar pleaded, holding his hands together as if in prayer.

The soldier shook a long finger in my face, "You are spies!"

"Spies, that's ridiculous. Can I ask you a question? Do I look like a spy? I am traveling to Kalendestine to deliver peace flags from my school in America. Now, if you don't mind we need to be on our way." I looked at Mr. Clark and he was so pale I thought he might be sick. He held his fingers to his lips signaling me to be quiet.

The soldier turned and walked back to the big truck, unlatched the back flap and ten more soldiers bounded from the truck, each carrying a gun. At the big soldier's order the others surrounded our jeep and pointed their guns directly at us. Fredrick flew to the top of the nearest tree observing the scene below, while Kool Kat watched just inside the forests' edge. I nodded to them signaling that it would be okay, but I was shaking inside.

Could this have been a huge mistake? Did I travel all this way to be turned back, or worse be held captive by men who clearly were not reasonable? We had always been taught to give and receive love from everyone. Again, I could hear Father's words, "Karen, always know where the exit door is in any situation." I needed the calm wisdom and assurance of Father at that moment, but in his absence, I leaned closer to Mr. Clark who placed a hand on my back and patted me gently. I thought, Now what do I do, Dad – there's no exit door in sight; no where to run. I then remembered and could hear and feel my Mother's voice saying "Pray, Karen." So I did. And it really worked! Phew!

"We'll be okay, little Miss. Just don't make them angrier," Mr. Clark said as he bent down to whisper in my ear.

"Okay, I'm sorry," I said and meant it.

The big soldier walked to Mr. Clark, grabbed his arm, pushed his coat sleeve up and said, "What color your skin?"

"What?" Mr. Clark answered, puzzled.

"Tell me, what color your skin ...her skin?" pointing at me.

"White, we are white," Mr. Clark answered matter-of-factly.

"Yes, white and we are not. You not like us, don't feel, think, live like us. You are enemy of all people not like you, yes?"

"No," Mr. Clark said trying to remain calm. "The young lady and I have no bias toward you. We have many friends and colleagues of different color in our country."

"Well, perhaps we have problem with you – your skin so white, you look like 'spheras'." Later I would learn that word in his language meant ghosts. The other soldiers thought that was hilarious because they all started laughing.

"Yes, you look sick, like spheras!"

Suddenly, I knew what it felt like to be hated and ridiculed for the color of my skin; a feeling I had never felt before; like I did not count and was completely at their mercy. For the first time in my life I realized what others, even in my own country, had felt countless times before. I experienced racial prejudice. It made me feel deeply sad and hurt. Most of all, it made me more afraid than I had ever been. I was so vulnerable. It truly felt like I was in a life-or-death situation. I did, however, know that somehow I would be okay.

At one point a very small mean looking man with a scary look, whom I had not noticed before, came toward me. He spoke "chitty chat" then, pulled me aside to show me something and there was a ledge with a drop about a mile long. The man smiled cruelly as he pointed over the ledge. I think he was hoping to frighten me enough that I would fall off the ledge. He seemed surprised that I maintained my footing and ran back to Mr. Clark! Good thing I have excellent balance!

I heard a familiar sound, high up in the tree. Kool Kat was meowing loudly as he scampered to my side. Fredrick fluttered close to my shoulder and whispered, "Be brave, Karen."

Kool Kat added in his softest cat voice, "We are close by – we will not leave you." Then they quickly moved again toward the trees, just before a nearby soldier had a chance to shoo them away.

The soldiers ordered us to sit on the ground and be silent as they began to search the jeep. I looked over my shoulder to the left and realized we were sitting just inches away from the edge of the road. One tiny misstep and any one of us could have fallen from the narrow ledge to the valley floor a mile below. One of the soldiers kept making us move closer and closer to the ledge, again, frightening us with the possibility of falling over the side.

The soldiers ripped out the seats of Genespar's jeep to look underneath them, they opened the hood and also searched underneath the car. Then, finally they took our bags from the back and emptied the contents out onto the road. My clothes, which had been carefully packed by Mother, now lay strewn all over the road. A brand new white sweater with pearl buttons was being trampled by the boots of a soldier as he sifted through everything. Mr. Clark was trying to keep important papers dumped from his brief case from flying away into the night. The papers included letters to the principal of the school, travel itineraries, airline tickets.

Then I saw them; the box holding the peace flags. It was off to the side and hadn't been noticed by the soldiers. I scooted slowly toward the box, hoping my movements would not be seen. I was going to try and hide the box behind me somehow. Too late! A soldier spotted the small box, walked over and roughly kicked it sending it several feet to the other side of the road. Then he picked it up, opened the top and turned the box upside down. The peace flags came tumbling out. Even though they were attached to each other, the wind swirled them into disarray and I was so afraid they would be torn and ruined. "Please," I shouted, "those are very important. Please, be careful."

He mimicked my look of concern, and was just about to rip the first flag from the cord when suddenly a familiar form appeared. Fredrick appeared out of nowhere and flew straight into the soldier's face causing him to drop the cord with the flags attached. Then, as the mean soldier tried to reach for it again, Kool Kat pounced on the soldier's leg and reached with his paw to take hold of the cord. As Kool Kat ran back toward the forest, the flags fanned out and the wind picked them up and the flags flew higher and higher into the air. It was a beautiful sight to see the flags all strung out together like that flying through the air, but I was so afraid the cord would break and the flags would be scattered far and wide. But the cord held as Kool Kat followed Fredrick's lead and took the flags safely away deep into the forest. I was giving them a thumbs up when Genespar started shouting to us.

"He now wants money ... give him any moneys

you have!"

Mr. Clark quickly turned over his wallet. The soldier took the cash and threw the credit cards to the ground. Genespar gave up the small amount of money he was carrying, then, they searched my purse, too and found only a few dollars in my wallet.

Then, it was over. As if some unheard signal was sent, the soldiers who had terrorized us for the last few minutes, ran to the tarp-covered truck, jumped in and the truck roared down the mountain and left us standing in the road.

Had that really happened? Did I dream it? I was still shaken as I began to retrieve my belongings scattered on the road. "Mr. Clark," I called out nearly in tears, "how can we continue on with no money?"

"Ah, they didn't get all of our money, Miss. Look!" He picked up his small black shaving kit tossed aside by the soldiers. Walking toward me he showed me the inside hidden pocket in the top of the kit. "See, here is where most of the money was all along. We are okay. And Genespar, we will make sure to repay the money you lost tonight as well. Everything is fine, even if they had taken all of our money," he said, as he laughed hard and long.

I was glad to see that Mr. Clark could not only smile, but laugh, as well. "I just hope the flags are okay, too," I commented to them both.

Then, Genespar was pointing to the sky with a huge smile, "Look there."

Coming through the forest Kool Kat emerged, still holding one end of the cord with the flags in his mouth, while Fredrick flew high with the other end tucked safely under his wing. Kool Kat guided him in for the landing. The flags fell in a neat pile at my feet. I was overjoyed. "Fredrick and Kool Kat, how can I thank you? That was the bravest, smartest thing I've ever seen."

Mr. Clark and Genespar were astounded at the feat of the two tiny creatures. "Miss, that is no ordinary cat and butterfly," Mr. Clark said.

"Oh, I've known that for a long time, Mr. Clark," as I carefully folded the last peace flag into place and closed the box's lid.

We loaded up again and with Genespar wiping his brow, we were all grateful that we had escaped harm as the jeep's engine revved to life. We had been taught a powerful lesson. Racial prejudice of any kind is cruel and painful. I silently prayed that we would cross into Kalendestine with no further encounters. I had seen first-hand how fearful and terrible even the threat of war can be.

Kool Kat and Fredrick nestled together in the carrier and as we drove through the night I thought of the children in Kalendestine who needed our messages of peace and hope. My eyes became so heavy and I fell asleep listening to Mr. Clark and Genespar go on and on, discussing their favorite foods. Seaweed was their main choice for their edible taste bud discussions!

THE MOST BEAUTIFUL SIGHT EVER!

Just before midnight we arrived at a small inn on the outskirts of Corinza. I changed into my pajamas then Mr. Clark knocked on my door to make sure I was safe and secure before giving me a goodnight hug. "Little Miss, we have been through a lot today. Sleep well, tomorrow will be a big day. I have called your parents to let them know we have safely arrived and that you will be speaking with them tomorrow. I did not find it necessary to tell them we were held at gunpoint today. They can learn of that episode when we return home. Agreed?"

I nodded in the affirmative. After he closed the door and checked that it was locked, I yawned and with Kool Kat stretched out at the foot of my bed and Fredrick resting atop the head board, I said a prayer before closing my eyes, "Dear God, thank you for protecting us today. Use me and the peace flags to show the children of Kalendestine they are loved and that kids in America care what happens to them. Help all go according to plan. Amen."

"Amen," said Fredrick.

"Me, too," meowed Kool Kat while closing his eyes one at a time.

I awoke early the next morning to the sound of

raining pelting the window. The downpour was so heavy that when I pulled the curtain back to take a look outside, I couldn't even make out the surroundings. Oh, no, I thought, this might cancel the flag ceremony at the school. I had an hour and a half to dress, have a bite of breakfast and head to the school. Fredrick and Malibu Kool Kat and I joined Mr. Clark, Genespar and the kind couple who were our hosts, for breakfast; hot tea with toast, spread with a tasty plum-like jam. I shared small bites with Fredrick and Kool Kat. It was delicious.

It was still raining when I loaded the boys back into their carrier and reached for the box with the peace flags. We climbed aboard the jeep once more for the short ride over to Corinza Secondary Government School, which sat in a busy section of town and could easily have been mistaken for a two-story office building. The first thing I noticed when we arrived were the four armed guards at the gated entrance to the school. A very tall man with a big mustache and a short woman with dark hair pulled back into a tight bun welcomed us, holding umbrellas to help keep us dry. Mr. Clark took the box holding the flags from me as I stepped down from the jeep. I would learn that the man, Mr. Malik, was the school's principal and the lady was a reporter with the state-owned newspaper, on site to cover the event. Once inside, Mr. Malik said to me in English, "The children are very excited to meet you, Miss Karen. However, the rain may keep us from having the flag event outdoors; but instead, we can do it in the auditorium."

My heart sank a little, "I understand," I said. We had planned for the peace flags to be displayed outside, waving beautifully in the wind. "We will have fun with what we have!"

Mr. Clark knew I was disappointed, but he encouraged me. "You know Miss, the important thing is that we are here and you cared enough to present the flags in person."

Just as we entered a hallway leading to the auditorium to greet the students, a loud alarm sounded throughout the building. It was almost deafening as I grabbed my ears. "Hurry, hurry – this way," Mr. Malik shouted as he ushered us through the hallway. We followed him into a room where we were instructed to sit down on the floor in a fetal position and cover our heads with our hands.

"It's a bomb alert," the lady reporter said to me. "Sadly, they are common occurrences."

"Yes, our students are used to taking such precautions often due to the enemy's bombing raids," the principal said shaking his head. I imagined all of the kids in the school having to do what I was doing at that moment. The alarm finally went off after what seemed like several minutes.

"It's all clear, Miss. We can now proceed," Mr. Malik said, but my ears were still ringing.

I won't lie. I was shaking when I asked, "You

mean your enemy would bomb the school on purpose, knowing there were students here?"

"Well, it may not be on purpose, but they target many places nearby and a bomb could go astray and we would be hit. They have come alarmingly close to the school," Mr. Malik said.

I couldn't imagine going to school every day fearing that a bomb could destroy my school and that lives could be lost. I was dwelling on that when I gathered myself and picked up the carrier holding Kool Kat and Fredrick. The look in their little eyes said they had been very frightened, too.

Then, I noticed Fredrick flitting frantically around in the carrier trying to get my attention. I held the carrier up to my ear and he whispered, "Karen, look, look out the window!" The rain had stopped and the sun was peaking through some low hanging clouds. "You can have the ceremony outside," he added.

I giggled as we walked toward the door of the auditorium. Mr. Malik opened the door and let me enter first. Suddenly, four hundred students who had already gathered there began to applaud. I was surprised! Smiles and happiness on the children's faces! Plus, it made me feel so happy to see how excited they were to share peace! All the children were giving me the peace sign and were hugging me as we walked through the crowd. Indeed, people everywhere want love and peace. I was directed to the stage area where two microphones had been attached to two microphone stands.

"Miss, please greet the students and tell them why you have come. We have an interpreter who will tell the children what you are saying," said Mr. Malik kindly.

I walked to one of the microphones while Mr. Clark sat the box of flags beside me. The lady reporter was taking pictures and then pulled out a note pad as I began to speak.

"Good morning, everyone!" I started. Then, waited for the interpreter who was a teacher at the school to repeat it.

"Good morning!" they echoed back in English. I smiled broadly before going on. "I have come a long way to bring something to you. In this box are pictures drawn by students at my school in the USA." Then I waited for the interpreter.

Suddenly in response to that comment, the lively students began to chant, "USA! USA!"

"These are more than pictures," I said when they were silent again. "They represent our hopes and prayers for you as you have to be strong and have courage everyday because of the unrest going on all around you. I wanted to see you in person to tell you that far away across the ocean there are kids just like you who care and want your leaders to find the way to peace. We call the pictures "peace-flags" and in a moment we will go wave them as a sign to all, that love and peace is the answer; not hate and war."

After the interpreter spoke, the students erupted again in waves of applause and cheers.

I stepped back from the microphone so Mr. Malik could give the children directions as to what would take place next. Then, I led the entire group up two flights of stairs to the top of the building which was a large, flat rooftop. When we arrived there, I let Kool Kat and Fredrick out of the carrier. They were elated to flit around the children gathering on the roof. Fredrick whispered close, "Well done, Karen. This is an exciting day."

Then, Kool Kat smoothed my legs from behind, as if to say, "Karen, take a look behind you."

Turning to the west I saw the most beautiful full rainbow arching across the deep blue sky. It formed the perfect backdrop as we proceeded. Like crystals, the rainbow's colors glistened in the sun streaming through the clouds. I sighed deeply and noticed Mr. Clark was approving the beautiful rainbow by giving me a "thumbs up" sign.

"You know, Karen, rainbows are recognized around the world as a sign of peace and hope," Fredrick said as he landed on Kool Kat's head.

From the box, one student took the first flag and walked to the far end of the roof top, then one by one, the students helped to stretch out the cord holding the flags until from one end of the roof to the other the flags were extended above their heads. As the reporter snapped pictures I took my place in the center with

Kool Kat and Fredrick helping me hold a sign we had brought along that read, "From Students in America - to Students of Kalendestine – Flags of Peace and Love."

As the flags flapped in the wind, the students decided to form a circle still holding the flags high. I took my place in the center and as my eyes went around the circle looking at the beautiful art work of my classmates back home, my heart swelled with pride. The student's laughter and joy brought tears to my eyes. "We did it!" I shouted to Kool Kat and Fredrick who were themselves circling around and around the children holding the flags. A television crew had joined us to record the happy spectacle.

The entire day was the greatest experience of my life. After eating lunch with the students and hearing about their country, I was interviewed by the lady reporter. She said the interview would be part of the evening news that would be aired across Kalendestine. She also said the story would be picked up by international networks as well. "You mean my parents and the kids and teachers back home could see the story?"

"Yes, that is very possible," she smiled warmly. She asked about my home, my family, our town of Summit and my school. She wanted to know how I came up with the idea for the peace flags. I answered every question, but the most difficult question was this one: "How can students your age in America possibly understand what our student's in Kalendestine endure

PEACE
UNITY
WAR ENDS! SOON
FROM USA KINDNESS
WITH L♥VE -YOUR AMERICAN FRIENDS

everyday because of the threats of war?"

After thinking about my answer for a moment, I said, "Honestly, I don't think we can know how your students feel, but we can let them know we care and encourage them to be strong. One day we hope they can live in peace and freedom once more. We pray that day comes very soon. It is wonderful to know that there are big-hearted, full of love children here in Kalendestine, just like in our country. I will continue to send light and love to you and your whole country."

She replied "Peace starts with one person and it is inside of you."

The interview and the video from the peace flag ceremony at the school was carried by all international news agencies that evening. The next morning Mr. Clark told me that many back home were calling to say they had seen me on television and that they were so proud of me. I was so excited to hear that the students saw their flags being flown. It felt so good to know we had made a small difference in the lives of some very terrific kids on the other side of the world.

Then, Mr. Clark told me the most awesome news. "Karen, the Mayor of New York City has left word that he wants you to come to New York when you return home. He has a special award he wants to present to you."

"Really, Mr. Clark? Oh, my goodness – I don't know what to say."

"Say, yes, silly ... say, yes!" Fredrick said.

A SPECIAL INVITATION TO NEW YORK CITY

Late that evening I spoke to my parents for the first time since arriving in Kalendestine. They were elated to tell me they had seen me on the news. "Karen, we are so proud of you. The whole town is talking about how brave you are to make such a trip. We can hardly wait for you to come home and tell us everything," Mom said.

Dad added, "You know, Karen, your idea of the peace flags has touched so many people. In fact, other organizations and student groups are making their own flags, hoping to deliver them to different people around the globe. Good for you, dear. Good for you!"

"Thanks, Dad, but wait until you hear this. The Mayor of New York City wants me to come to New York as soon as possible! He has an award for me."

"That is wonderful, Karen! We will rebook your flight home and have you flown directly into New York City and your Mother and I will meet you there when you arrive?"

"I love that idea!"

"Okay, I will send Mr. Clark the details for you."

Then, Mom asked, "How are Fredrick and Kool Kat doing? Did they have an exciting time, too?"

"Oh, yes…they were perfect gentlemen," I answered.

"Everyone they meet loves them immediately."

We finished our phone conversation and then Genespar gassed up the jeep to make the trip back down the mountain to the Kalendestine Airport. As we rode along I carried so many wonderful memories in my heart. I whispered, "Oh, Fredrick and Kool Kat, how I wish everyone who created a peace flag could have been with us to see how happy we made those students today."

Wise and insightful as ever, Fredrick answered, "Well, you could invite them to New York City to share the Mayor's award."

"What a great idea, Fredrick! I'll call the school as soon as we get to the airport. Miss Johnson can let the students know about the Mayor's special invitation. Anyone who can join us will be welcome to attend the award celebration with me. After all, it took all of us, working together to create those wonderful flags; all special friends like Rebecca Hasbrouck, Linda Jane Kerkhan aka "Kerby" Ferling and my Summit High School class must come!

My heart became heavy as I said goodbye to our friend and driver, Genespar, at the airport. I thought I saw a little tear in his eye as he said, "Miss Karen, we have had many adventures in our short time together. My hope would be that one day we will meet again. You have a brave and pure heart. I would be honored to drive you anywhere if ever needed again."

I hugged his neck, "Oh, Genespar, you kept us

protected and you are so fun! I will miss your happy whistling and the way you are always willing to help. I love you and thank you.”

“No, no thank you little Miss … you have given me many happy memories. I will miss your Mr. Fredrick and Mr. Kool Kat, too. Hooray, for peace and hooray for the U.S.A.!”

He and Mr. Clark shook hands and then we watched Genespar drive away waving to us until he was out of sight. Fredrick lifted a wing to wave goodbye and Kool Kat meowed and nodded to Genespar, too.

While waiting for our flight out I connected by phone with Miss Johnson and told her about the Mayor’s invitation to New York City. “It would be great if you and some of the kids could be there for the ceremony. Please let them know the time and place. I would love to share the award with them.” She said she would pass the information along as soon as possible.

After boarding our plane, Mr. Clark and I sat together and talked about the wonderful experiences we shared over the last few days. He even confessed how frightened he had been when the soldiers held us captive for those few minutes. “There I was, hired to protect you, and I could do nothing. I was very concerned for all of us,” he shared.

“Mr. Clark, I can only imagine how I would have felt without you there. You were cool and calm the whole time. Thank you." He has turned out to be a wonderful, caring friend.

After the long flight, Mother and Father met us as we exited the plane in New York City. They hugged me tight and continually told me how proud they were of me. I could hardly wait to tell them about our adventures in Kalendestine, but I was also very tired from the long plane ride. So, they let me nap in the taxi over to the Plaza Hotel where we would spend the next couple of nights. There would be plenty of time to catch up later. Fredrick and Kool Kat nestled close together in the carrier, clearly tired from traveling, too.

"You will be so pleased to know that Miss Johnson let us know that there will be several of your classmates at the ceremony tomorrow at the Mayor's office, Karen. Miss Johnson will be there, too. They are very excited," Mom told me in the elevator ride up to our suite at the beautiful Plaza Hotel. We had stayed at The Plaza on 5th Avenue many times when visiting the city so I was familiar with the hotel and knew we would have a beautiful room overlooking Central Park. Before retiring to his room, Mr. Clark said goodnight and he even bent down close to say to Kool Kat and Fredrick, "Sleep well, little friends. We have another big day tomorrow."

I smiled at that thought.

The next morning my parents and I had breakfast downstairs at the famous Plaza Tea Room. When I returned to the suite to dress for the award presentation, Fredrick and Kool Kat were both hiding behind the couch in my room. "Hey, what are you guys doing back there?"

I heard laughter and then Fredrick flew in sight followed by Kool Kat darting out from behind the sofa. I was so surprised and delighted! They had both created little tuxedos from the large black and white paper napkins available in the hotel bathroom. "Oh my goodness," I said, "you both look great!" Kool Kat even had fashioned a top hat that sat smartly on his head.

"Well, Karen, we wanted to look presentable for your big day. How do we look?" Fredrick said as he spread his wings wide and puffed out his body showing off his "tux."

"You both look wonderful and how clever of you! I want a picture of all of us after I am ready to go." Then, I dashed to put on the dress Mother had brought along for me to wear to the ceremony. It was white with yellow daisies embroidered on the skirt. I combed my hair and added a yellow ribbon to finish the look. "How pretty you look, Karen," Dad said as he offered his arm to escort me down the hall to the elevator.

"And your friends look great, too!" Mother said, nodding toward Fredrick and Kool Kat who followed behind looking very elegant indeed. Mr. Clark met us in the lobby so we could all taxi over to New York City's City Hall where the office of the Mayor was located.

Just before we exited the hotel we paused for

a picture in the lobby. It was then that I caught a glimpse of a little girl, around six-years-old. She smiled widely from behind a large marble pillar, then quickly disappeared. Where did she go, I wondered, as we passed through the revolving door of the hotel. Looking back over my shoulder I saw her again. She had blonde hair and a mischievous look in her eyes as she waved to me from the large stair case that descends into the Plaza dining room. She was dressed in pink and black with a cute little dog following her every step. Wait a minute, I thought, that's Eloise.

When I was younger, I had read all the books about Eloise, the girl who lived on the "tippy-top" floor of the Plaza Hotel. She lived there with her nanny, her dog, Weenie, and a pet turtle named Skipperdee. Her adventures had enchanted me and I whispered to Fredrick and Kool Kat, "Boys, that was Eloise; she lives here at The Plaza. Maybe we can find her later and have a cup of tea together. She is so cute!"

The room where the press conference was to take place was on the 3rd floor of City Hall. It was a huge room with a stage at one end. Several microphones were in place and chairs set out for the audience were filling up. Then I saw them, standing to the side of the platform. I broke into a run and with hugs-a-plenty I greeted the twenty or more students with Miss Johnson who had made the trip from Summit to be with me on this special day "You guys! Thanks for coming," I said, "now, when the Mayor calls me up

I'm going to ask you all to come up, too, so be ready."

"Karen, we are so proud of you and the whole town wants you to come home so we can celebrate your trip to Kalendestine, too," Miss Johnson offered.

"Sure. But, we did it together … right guys?" The kids cheered and then took their seats as a tall, distinguished looking man with white hair stepped into the room. I took my place on the podium along side my parents who were beaming with pride the whole time. When I was seated, Fredrick came to rest on my shoulder and Kool Kat hopped up to nestle in my lap.

The tall man walked directly to where we were sitting, extended his hand to me and said, "So, this must be Karen. Karen, I am the Mayor and I want you to know that you, young lady, are just what this country needs. You are a person who cares and found a way to show it. We are all very proud of you and in a moment I will share a few words and then present you with an award of appreciation. Thank you so much for coming, I think it is fair to say the world adores you."

"Thank you, Mr. Mayor. These are my parents, Mr. and Mrs. Smythe. And these are my friends, Fredrick and Kool Kat. It is an honor to be here, sir. "

He shook my parents' hands, nodded toward Fredrick and Kool Kat, then, patted my shoulder before walking to the microphone to speak: "Ladies and Gentlemen, we are here today because one young girl from Summit had an idea; an idea that would help others in a country far away from our safe shores. She got her classmates involved and soon she was on her way to Kalendestine to deliver a wonderful message of hope and peace."

While the Mayor was speaking, the screen behind us began to show pictures of the kids in Kalendestine holding up the peace flags from the rooftop of the school. The slides showed the rainbow behind them glowing beautifully against the steel-blue sky. The Mayor continued, "What Karen did has inspired thousands of us who saw the happy faces of these students holding up peace flags created by Karen and her classmates, some who are present today." At that, everyone applauded and looked toward the area where my classmates sat. "So, Miss Karen, would you join me please? And I think you wanted your school friends and a very special teacher to join you as well. And you have two other special friends, a butterfly named Fredrick and a cat appropriately named Malibu Kool Kat, who accompanied you on your trip. I'm sure you want them to join you, too."

I rose from my chair and motioned for Fredrick and Kool Kat to follow me to the platform. The kids and Miss Johnson from Summit High piled onto the stage and stood in a semi-circle behind the Mayor and me. Fredrick and Kool Kat stood at attention at my feet. The Mayor took from a box a beautiful sky blue ribbon holding a gold medallion. He said, "In honor of your service to our country and in promotion of peace around the world I award you, Miss Karen Smythe, the Mayor's Humanitarian Peace Award." Then he slipped the ribbon around my neck and I beamed as the audience cheered. Then the Mayor's assistant began to pass to each student on the stage a lovely pin to commemorate their contribution to the flag mission, too. "Karen, would you like to speak to the audience?"

I hesitated for a moment, then, Fredrick whispered, "Yes, you do. Go on, Karen. At least, say thank you."

I winked at Fredrick as I said, "I was planning on saying 'thank you' and expressing my gratitude; of course, I will." I stepped to the microphone while pictures were being taken by many in the room. "First, I want to say to the Mayor and the city, thank you so much for this honor. I'm just one person, a teenager from a small town, but, you never know when an idea you have can brighten a life, or make a difference for someone else. The peace flags were our way of saying anyone can get involved to deliver an important message; even half way around the world. I will treasure this moment for the rest of my life. Thanks to Fredrick and Malibu Kool Kat and thanks also to Miss Johnson and my classmates from Summit High for helping!"

When I mentioned our school the kids cheered loudly. It was great. The Mayor then thanked everyone for coming and dismissed the crowd. Afterward, Father spoke to Miss Johnson and my classmates, "If you have time please join us back at The Plaza for a small reception. We'd love to have you if you don't have to get back to Summit right away."

"That would be lovely, Mr. Smythe. I will let the students know. I will be joining you there for sure," she said.

ON OUR OWN IN NYC

The Mayor's office had graciously arranged for two large limousines to pick us up in front of City Hall and return us to the Plaza for the reception. I was busy talking to reporters and posing for photographs with Kool Kat and Fredrick when Dad called to me, "Karen, we will take this limo. You take the other with Kool Kat and Fredrick and we will meet you back at the hotel. The driver knows where to go."

"Okay, Dad. See you in a few minutes," I shouted to him across the way. Several moments passed as I was telling one reporter after another about the peace flags and the mission to Kalendestine. I had just finished one conversation when Fredrick nudged me with a wing, "Karen, our driver just left us." I had been so distracted that I hadn't seen the limo we were supposed to take pull away, leaving us behind. Suddenly I panicked, "Oh, no. I do not have my purse with me, no money to take a cab. What are we going to do?" The City Hall was located in the Battery Park area of New York City and The Plaza Hotel was miles away in mid-town. I turned to Kool Kat and Fredrick for ideas.

"What about the subway?" Fredrick said. "We can see if the ticket person will give us a ticket. Perhaps if we explain what happened they will help us out."

"That's a good idea, Fredrick. Let's try it." We

descended the stairs into the nearby subway station. A sign with an arrow read: To Manhattan, Central Park. I knew of course, that the Plaza was situated next to Central Park. "That's the train we need to take." I walked to the booth where a lady was selling tickets to ride the subway. She was stern looking and seemed as though she was not having a good day. In my friendliest voice I said, "Hello, Ma'am, I am visiting New York City and my parents took a car and the car I was to take left me. They didn't know I would be needing any money, so, could you possibly help me out and give me a subway ticket to Manhattan, please."

"Heard it before, kid. Nope – not going to happen. You and your strange pets, step aside. Next!" she called out, cutting me off before I could explain further.

"How very rude," Kool Kat said shooting her a dirty look.

"Boys, we have to think. There are people waiting for us at The Plaza. Do you see any loose change on the ground?" We scoured the area looking for coins that had been dropped by hurried travelers. There was nothing, not one penny.

"Karen, look over there at that young fellow playing the violin; people are dropping money into a hat nearby. Maybe we can do the same."

"Well, I don't have a violin, Fredrick, and I certainly couldn't play it if I had one, but ... wait a minute. Perhaps, people would stop to watch a butterfly and a cat do some tricks and I can sing and dance with you, too! Wow, I mean that's something they wouldn't see every day. Come on, boys, I have a plan."

I found a discarded soda cup to catch coins and situated myself not far from the main descending stairway. Mustering some confidence, I announced with a loud voice, "Ladies and Gentlemen, now presenting Malibu Kool Kat and Fredrick the Butterfly to amaze you with special skills and tricks. If you enjoy them today please help us out by dropping a few coins in our cup. First, Malibu Kool Kat …."

As if on cue, men, women, boys and girls began to stop and wait for what was coming next. I motioned for Kool Kat to begin his act. He scurried to one of the subway pillars, then, jumping up with all fours, he began to climb all the way nearly to the subway ceiling. Then, he let out a blood-curdling meow before plummeting to the floor below with legs spread out like a parachute. Then, he landed on the ground on his four paws, light as a feather and offered a mischievous smile as he stuck his tail straight up in the air. People applauded and looked amazed at the agile cat's feat and most of them tossed a few coins into the cup before walking on.

I continued immediately, "Now, Fredrick The Butterfly will amaze you with his precision flying while dancing to "The Nutcracker Suite". I began to hum the tune and dance while Fredrick, gracious as ever, swooped and spiraled and created beautiful movements to the music. Then, I beckoned him to land on my shoulder at the finish. Again, the people who stopped to watch were amazed and contributed more coins in the cup. We went through each act three more times before I stopped to count the money in the cup.

"Boys, look – we have $4.25. The ticket is $3.00; we have enough money for the subway ticket and even some left over!"

I proudly walked to the same woman who had rejected us before, passed her the change and said, "One ticket to Manhattan station, please." She didn't even look up, but handed me a ticket. "We did it; thanks to you both; you were great!" I said as we boarded the train and took a seat to head toward mid-town.

We hurriedly rushed into The Plaza and went directly to the room Dad had reserved for the reception. When we entered Mom and Dad rushed to my side. He said, "Karen, we were worried sick. The limo driver said he thought you caught another ride and returned without you. Are you okay, dear?"

"I am great, Dad! I am having a blast!"

Dad said "That is good to hear."

Mom added, "Good for you."

"Yes, but we had quite an adventure. I'll tell you all about it later." I winked at Kool Kat and Fredrick who strutted about the crowd, acting like celebrities, still dressed in their homemade tuxedos. Then, I walked to the table for a glass of punch and a cookie and began visiting with all my Summit High friends who had made it over to the hotel from the award ceremony. Then I saw her – the same little girl I had seen earlier, as she peeked into the room and this time I called to her, "Hi, Eloise, come and meet my friends!"

Shyly she entered the room at first, but, then, just like a prima donna, she marched into the room and announced to everyone, "Thank you all for visiting me and my hotel today! I am Eloise and if you want to see my room later, I'd be happy to show you. Please continue to enjoy yourselves."

I smiled at her comments, then, made sure she had some treats. Eloise stayed until my guests departed. Then, she escorted me to her special room high atop The Plaza; a magical room all decked out in black and pink, her favorite colors. I met her dog and her turtle, too, and they enjoyed meeting Fredrick and Kool Kat. We sat in her parlor and became quick friends. She wanted to share a couple of her adventures with me and, oh, boy, I had a few I wanted to tell her about, too. Before saying goodnight, I promised to visit her again on my next stay at The Plaza. Eloise really is a great little kid.

Later that evening, I filled Mom and Dad in on our subway adventure. They were amazed and grateful that we had used our gifts and instincts to find our way to The Plaza. As I reached to turn off the lamp on the night stand, Fredrick lighted on top of the bed stand, "You know, Karen, I think I could use a little less drama for a few days."

I agreed, "I know. But we sure have made lots of cool memories to think about."

Kool Kat had already found a cozy spot on a pillow tossed onto a nearby chair and was fast asleep. "Fredrick, thank you for being such a great friend," I added, leaning my head back onto the pillow.

"Yes, we are forever friends. Goodnight, Karen."

"Goodnight, Fred ...er ...." I had already drifted off to sleep.

OUR ISLAND ESCAPADE

I returned to Summit to finish out the school year. Everyone wanted to hear more about the Kalendestine trip. I spoke to our school in a special assembly and the newspaper also printed a follow-up article about the trip under the headline: "Peace Flags: A Success in Kalendestine!" Because of all the media coverage, everyone in Summit seemed to know who I was and townspeople of all ages would stop to say something nice anytime I was out and about. The biggest stars, however, seemed to be Fredrick and Kool Kat. Younger kids especially wanted to meet them. Those two loved being famous. Kool Kat even started wearing black rimmed sunglasses around town; as if he was being followed by paparazzi. That funny cat!

When school was out for the summer, the family planned a vacation to Caye Caulker Island in Belize, a country south of Mexico in the Caribbean Sea. We arrived to discover beautiful white, sandy beaches and a laid-back way of life that we all embraced right away, especially Fredrick and Kool Kat. We were renting a nice condo on the beach, but, then Father proposed a plan. "You know, Karen, if you really want to experience island life, there is a group operating a camp for young people here on the island." He reached across the table to pick up a bright colored brochure he'd picked up that morning. "The kids there work together to grow their own vegetables, they fish for food, sleep on the beach, on beds they make from palm leaves. They also make their own bread, and even make the sugar they use. It may be the makings of another grand adventure for you if you wanted to join them."

I was already a little bored, so the idea of being around kids my own age for a few days sounded great so, I said, "Sure, Dad – sign me up!"

I almost changed my mind when Dad took me down to the beach to meet the camp director that afternoon. His name was Mr. Slagle and he was sweeping out one of the shacks used to house the campers. It was not much more than four walls. There was a bathroom with a primitive shower stall behind the Main Fort (which they called the main meeting area).

"Hi, Karen," the middle-aged bald man said pleasantly. "Well, now, all you have is cold water here for bathing. And, at night the lightening bugs will light up your room and that will be your only electricity! We sleep in hammocks and to cook we build a fire in the fire pit and use sea shells as dishes! I'm just getting this hut ready; we have five more like this one on the property. Three are girls' cabins and three more for the guys. Are you thinking of joining the camp for a few weeks?"

It all sounded wonderful to me! "Yes," I said, then

watched the biggest red ant I'd ever seen crawl out from under Mr. Slagle's broom.

"Oh, that ant is a fire ant and can sting you," Mr. Slagle said matter-of-factly. Then he continued, "The rules are listed on that brochure there on the table. Here at Camp Caulker we get up early and go to bed early; in between we work hard, but we also play hard. We make sure there's lots of free time, too, but there are no televisions or radios, or phones. We have flares we can send up as signals in case of emergency - so far we have not had to use them.

"We have a boat that comes in once a month. In the meantime we pick fruit and catch fish to eat! We have a protected environment here, monitored for safety 24/7 and we guarantee memories to last a lifetime. We have kids that come for the whole summer, then, some are here for only two weeks, or a month. And they come from all over – America, Britain, Mexico, Honduras. That sound interesting to you?"

I started to answer when he added, "Oh, and you will learn to meditate along with different spiritual people from Tahiti and with real Tibetan monks. We pray like you do and we keep the peace. Remember, to keep being kind to yourself; it's a purpose!" Mr. Slagle ended his comments with a smile.

Interesting, I thought. I looked at Father before I answered. He said, "It's your decision, Karen. Of course, we will be close by if needed, but it could be the makings of a life-changing summer for you. Your call, "Sweetie"

Before I knew it, I said, "Okay, I'll try it for two weeks. One quick question, though, Mr. Slagle. I have a very well behaved cat named Kool Kat and a butterfly friend, Fredrick. Could they come to Camp Caulker with me?"

"Well, we usually don't allow for pets, but if they don't cause any trouble or become too noisy at night I think it will be fine. Just let us know if you want to stay longer than two weeks. That can be arranged easily."

I was handed paper-work to fill out and Dad gave Mr. Slagle a check for my two weeks stay at Camp Caulker.

"Your move-in will be next Sunday night and on Monday morning we will show you the ropes around here. It will be great to have you, Karen, It may look rough, but we have kids who love it so much that they return to Camp Caulker year after year. We will look forward to getting to know you."

Walking back with Dad to our plush suite I thought about phrases the camp brochure had used to describe what I would be doing while at camp: "fishing for food … making bread … sleeping in a hammock on the beach." Well, I love simplicity and nature and interacting with different kinds of people (even if I could not speak their language), but I am not sure I am cut out for any of those activities, mainly because I've never tried them before. But, hey, I continued to think, I had never been to Kalendestine before either, or been held hostage by men with guns, or had to make money to get a subway ticket. I felt that at least I had to try it.

On Sunday evening, Dad walked me to Cabin #5 at the camp. He left me some spending money and told me to call him if I needed anything. Except there was no way to call! There were four girls already in the cabin and they had claimed the top bunks. I put my backpack and small suitcase on the bottom bunk next to the door. "Hi, I'm Anne Levine I'll be sleeping in the hammock next to you. The dark haired girl with short curly hair said in a very heavy southern accent.

I smiled, "I'm Karen. Where are you from?"

"Texas. Just outside of Dallas. This is my second summer to come to Camp Caulker. This really is the best girls' cabin. You know why? Because it is closest to the boys' cabins. We can prank them much easier from here."

I laughed, "Well, all right. Where do I put my stuff?"

"We stash our packs under the bed, mostly – there is a small closet over there, but most of us don't bring hang-up clothes."

"Okay," I answered while trying to fit my oversized backpack under the bed. I finally got it stored underneath then turned to meet the other girls in the room: Maria from Mexico City, Roberta from France (who asked me to call her, Bobbi), and, Mira, a tiny blond girl with braids, from Tahiti.

"Hey, who is this?" Bobbi asked when she spotted the carrier case holding Fredrick and Kool Kat sitting atop my bunk bed.

"This is Fredrick, the butterfly and that is Kool Kat." The girls squealed with delight when Fredrick flew out to make friends and Kool Kat slinked out of the carrier.

"This is the coolest deal ever, we'll have the only cabin with real live mascots…Fredrick and Kool Kat!" Anne said stroking Kool Kat's chin.

"That may be the most beautiful butterfly I have ever seen," shy Mira said, seemingly mesmerized by Fredrick's bright neon-like wings. "And, Malibu Kool Kat has a 'go with the flow' personality," Mira observed.

Later outside the cabin, native birds were singing as the girls and I learned new dances, sang native songs and shared our own made up songs while beating on hand made-drums and coconuts.

That night around a campfire all of us introduced ourselves before enjoying smores and hot chocolate. It was surprisingly cool with the ocean breezes whipping up the sand at our feet. The boys sat at one end of the fire and the girls at the other. One boy in particular caught my eye. He had sun-streaked blonde hair and sky-blue eyes and when he caught me looking at him he smiled a little boy smile and nodded in my direction.

"That's Micah Brandish," Anne whispered. "His family is very wealthy, from Ireland, I think. He is a champion soccer player already being scouted by the pros."

"Wow, impressive," I answered, before reaching for another marshmallow. "I'm a pretty good soccer player myself. I'll have to challenge him to a match."

"You're a brave girl. Go for it. He doesn't talk much, but maybe he'll talk to you."

And talk he did. Over the next couple of days Micah and I became inseparable. He told me about his parents who were divorced when he was 10-years-old. He loved his Dad, but hardly ever saw him, because he traveled so much with his business. His Mother was distant and sad most of the time. He felt closest to his Grandparents on his Father's side.

In turn, I told him about my home in Summit, my family, my adventures with the peace-flags and the New York trip. I even told him about the special abilities of Fredrick and Kool Kat. He thought it was all "very cool."

My closest friends had always been girls, but meeting Micah changed that. We just "got each other." We ate breakfast together, volunteered for the same work duty, swam together, and yes, challenged each other to one-on-one soccer matches. He even let me win a point now and then. Plus we went night snorkeling with underwater flashlights! I learned that lobsters only come out at night so we got to see the lobsters! Later, as we walked barefoot along the shore, I stepped on a porcupine needle. "Ouch!" I shouted hopping on one foot, "it really hurts!" As I stopped to pull the quill out, I lost my balance and landed face down in the sand. I was okay, but, Micah had a great laugh at my expense.

He took my teasing well, too, especially when I pointed out the dimple in his chin, "Why, that is the deepest dimple I have ever seen." That night we sat on the beach and talked about all the things we wanted to see and do before we were too old to do them.

One evening a day or two later, Micah was particularly quiet. "Something wrong Micah? You've hardly spoken all day."

"Ah, it's not a big deal. Just got a letter from my Dad today. He was supposed to meet me here after camp was over and we were going to travel to the states for some sight-seeing. But, his plans have changed and he says he can't even fly here to meet me. I'll have to return home alone."

"I'm sorry, Micah. I'm sure he'd be here if he could."

"Nah, I think he's too busy making more and more money. He's already made enough for five lifetimes. I'd rather have his time, then have all the stuff his money buys me."

"Have you told him that? Maybe he doesn't think you need him that much. Talking may help you both to find an inner peace."

"I've tried, but guess I could try again. It doesn't matter how rich you are, Karen. Some of the richest kids I know have no direction and aren't really happy,"

Micah seemed to grow sadder as he leaned against a rock and dug his bare toes into the sand.

I tried to lighten the mood, "Well, everyone has things to learn for our whole lives. You know, learning, staying fit by exercising, and only going to the best places with the best, "safest" people; even eating nutritious food - all of those things are important to do for the rest of our lives, but you know what," I added as I tousled his hair, "you have to think and do the things that make you happiest. Like helping other people, giving love and receiving love. You must take care of yourself and follow your heart and instincts. Be smart. Give your Dad another try. Now come on, I'll race you to the snack bar before it's closed."

Micah walked me to my cabin before lights out every evening and he made Fredrick and Kool Kat his pals from the beginning, even teaching them silly songs he'd learned as a child. They loved Micah. "Hey," I would remind them, "you can't like Micah more than me. I still feed you, you know." I was happy that the boys seemed to make Micah so happy, too.

One afternoon after our free time was spent snorkeling, a big yacht docked at the nearby pier. As Micah and I headed back to camp from the beach we met the owner of the yacht. He was a United States Senator from Florida. He invited us on board to look around and when we were leaving he said, "If you kids get tired from snorkeling tomorrow, climb inside the big rubber raft tied to the back of the boat to take a rest. Feel free to use it anytime."

"Thanks, sir. We just might do that," Micah answered for us.

The very next afternoon after all our camp chores were done, Micah and I went snorkeling again. It had been an absolutely beautiful day. We could see the waves crashing on the second largest coral reef in the world less than a mile away and we would stop now and then to watch the flying fish shooting up out of the water!

Sure enough, when we grew tired from swimming we remembered the senator's offer and climbed inside the raft attached to the big yacht. It was so warm and relaxing and with the rocking motion of the raft, we both soon fell asleep. I woke to Micah, shouting, "Karen, wake up. We're in trouble. The raft must have broken away from the boat while we slept and we've drifted far away!"

The first thing I thought of was the fact there were huge sharks in the waters. "What? Are you kidding? We're out on some coral reef, Micah. What are we going to do?"

"Man, I don't have any clue where we are. Our only hope is that someone on the senator's boat saw us in the raft and realizes that it broke away."

"I'm scared, Micah ... really scared."

"I am too. Let's not panic, though. Hey, the camp people will look for us, too, when we don't check in for dinner. Someone will come for us. They will."

I tried to believe that Micah was right, but as the afternoon sun slipped further down toward the horizon I couldn't pretend that I wasn't afraid. There was nothing but water surrounding us and the raft would not have provided much protection from a big wave or dangerous rocks that jutted out from the reef.

In an attempt to distract me, Micah said, "Okay, we're gonna play, 'Name That Tune' - I'll hum something and you try to tell me what the song is." He started humming ... badly. So badly, that it made me smile. I did finally pick up the melody line, "Is that supposed to be 'New York, New York'?"

"Yeah, you got it, smarty-pants. Okay, you try one."

My humming was no better, but after a few bars, Micah blurted out, "Is it 'The Star Spangled Banner'?"

"Oh, you know it was," I answered. We went on and on for several minutes, humming through some Beatle songs, Broadway hits, and just when I was getting into Elvis Presley's, 'Blue Suede Shoes', we heard a slight rustling noise above us. The tiny figure became clearer as it neared the raft.

"Oh my gosh, it's Fredrick! Down here, we're down here," I shouted waving my arms wildly. Fredrick landed on the raft and pointed a wing toward the shore. There excitedly wagging his tail and bobbing up and down was Kool Kat. Fredrick had directed him to our very spot. I was so happy to see them I was near tears. "How did you find us? I've been so scared."

Fredrick said calmly, "We knew something was

wrong when you didn't return from snorkeling in time for dinner. So, we found the yacht and caused an awful ruckus when we saw that your raft had become detached from the boat. The senator was notified and just about anytime now the Coast Guard is going to show up to carry you in to shore. But, we couldn't wait, so we've been searching for you, too. Are you both all right?"

"Yes, just getting a little hungry," I answered

"And, I was sure hoping I didn't have to hear Karen trying to hum one more song," Micah chided.

"Me? You are terrible," we laughed. "Boys, thanks is all I can say. I somehow knew you'd do something to help find us."

It wasn't long before a Coast Guard patrol boat pulled up and rescued us from the reef. Back at camp, Micah and I sat quietly eating the dinner the camp cook had held back for us. As camp food goes, it was delicious. It was nearly time for lights out when Micah walked me to the cabin. Before turning to go he said, "You know, Karen. You are a pretty cool girl. If I ever get stranded again, I hope it's with you."

"Well, thanks … I think," I said trying to sound funny, and then added, "Seriously, Micah, you were brave out there. Thanks for staying calm and hopeful and for being a great friend."

"Thanks, but, we owe Fredrick and Kool Kat, big-time, too."

Then, before I stepped through the door he reached

to hug me and I returned the hug. Thinking back on that hug - it was almost better than a first kiss. Micah held the hug until I let go.

"See you tomorrow. I'm beat!" he said.

"Me, too. G-night, Micah."

The cabin girls wanted to know every detail of the near disaster and we talked in whispers long after the lights went out. Kool Kat and Fredrick had fallen asleep at the foot of my bed, but I was wide awake. I could hardly believe that in two days I would be saying goodbye to these girls and other friends I'd made at Camp Caulker. And, how in the world was I going to say goodbye to Micah? I couldn't even imagine how hard that was going to be.

PARTY ON THE BEACH

It was the final night of my stay at Camp Caulker. My family and I would be returning home in the next few days. As usual, the camp director and staff hosted a "clambake" on the beach for the final night and there would be music and fun and games all evening. Parents were invited, too and also many of the local children showed up to share in the fun. I had gotten to know a few of the native children who would stop by to visit with the campers nearly every day. One afternoon in the activity hut, I had showed them how to make "peace flags." With paints and pencils they created their own flags as I told them about my special trip to Kalendestine. They were so proud of their flags.

As the sun was setting, splashing red and gold all along the horizon, my parents and I walked down to the party area and looked out to see tiny boats coming ashore with children from a nearby neighboring island dressed in colorful shirts and shorts. Fredrick and Kool Kat hung around nearby watching seagulls wading in and out of the tide. The clambake was on and a bon-fire was just getting started. A live band played while people danced and even took their turn doing the Limbo. Even the Senator who owned the yacht docked nearby showed up. Along with him were some movie stars that he had invited on to his boat. I couldn't believe it. That night I even met movie stars like Lauren Bacall and comedian Bill Murray and Ringo Starr of Beatles fame! Plus, there were aristocrats, diplomats, and philanthropists in the crowd; everyone you could imagine, plus, royalty like me. Ta da!

My parents were almost speechless when meeting such celebrities. Dad especially connected with Huntington Hartford, one of the wealthiest men in the world. Over the coming years, Mr. Hartford and I would become close friends. Another friend of the Senator owned a real castle in Ireland. In a heavy Irish brogue he said, "Young lady, I want you to come to my castle next month. I am hosting a party with the Rolling Stones! It is going to be a lovely time. Try to come, won't you? And bring along your little butterfly and the cat!"

I could only imagine making such a trip. (And, in fact, I did make the trip to Ireland and I would indeed stay in that castle, and yes, I even danced with Keith Richards himself! But, that was later.) For now I was enjoying the glorious sunset and the happy people dancing on the beach. As the sun was sinking further in the west, a horde of lightning bugs (fireflies) arrived to light up the beach with a mystic twinkling glow. It was then that I caught sight of Micah engaged in a conversation with an older man and the camp director. Could it be? I walked to his side and nudged his elbow.

Micah turned to me with a smile, "Karen, meet my Dad."

"Mr. Brandish! You made it. I'm so glad to see you. Does this mean you and Micah will be making the trip to the states?"

"Yes, we will, my dear. Micah told me that you encouraged him to call me and tell me exactly what he needed from me. I have been much too busy and and time is too short to not take every opportunity to be with my son. Thank you for that."

I blushed deeply. "I just know Micah loves you and needs you every day."

"Yeah, but right now I need to "boogie". Let's dance, Karen," Micah said as he grabbed my arm to lead me to the center of the crowd where we danced in the sand. I wanted to make time stand still and capture this memory exactly as it was happening. The evening was going way too fast.

Finally, it was time for farewells. I hugged the girls who had become great fun friends; I hugged Mr. Slagle and thanked him for the great time at camp; then I had to say goodbye to Micah. I motioned him to the edge of the bonfire as the music was dying away. I took his hand, "Micah, thank you for being such a great friend. I must say, I've never had an actual boy as a friend. After all, we were stranded at sea together. Doesn't that make us bonded for life?"

He laughed and hugged me. "Yes, we are. By the way, Dad and I plan on making a swing through

Summit before our trip to the states is over. Can we have a date?"

"Are you kidding? That would be awesome! You have my address and phone number, just let me know when you'll be there."

Before I knew it, Micah planted a kiss on my cheek. "That's for being the coolest, kindest girl I've ever met. And, you know how to have fun." Malibu Kool Kat and Fredrick flew in to say goodbye, too. "And you two – how could I forget you guys!"

Dad and Mom were already waving at me to come along. "Well, I've got to go. Goodbye for now, Micah. I'll see you in Summit. Enjoy your time with your Dad."

He gave me a wink and we parted. I ran to catch up with Mom and Dad.

Memorial Field in Summit, New Jersey

Other honors came when I returned home to Summit. The Summit Chamber of Commerce presented me with a beautiful plaque and named August 15th as "Karen Smythe, Keep The Peace Day". That was amazing! But the best was yet to come.

There is a small park within walking distance of my home in Summit. Memorial Field has a playground area with slides and a swing set. It also has a small plaza honoring men and women from Summit who have died serving in the military for our country. Every 4th of July, the veterans hold a memorial service in the quaint little plaza with stone benches along the outer edge. "Taps" is played and the names of the fallen are read aloud by the brave veterans who survived our nation's wars.

A few paces away from the plaza there is a small waterfall with natural stone retaining walls. Nestled off to one side, in a small alcove, is a statue carved from the bedrock found throughout the vicinity. I am so humbled each time I pass this way, because my city erected a statue in my honor. The statue is a girl joyfully looking up at the flag she holds overhead; a peace flag. Perched on her shoulders is a butterfly and sitting by her side is a black cat with a white patch of

"To Honor a young girl who followed her heart and dreamed a dream in the hope that people everywhere will choose to live in peace and harmony"
WORLD PEACE
PEACE
PEACE LOVE

fur over his heart. The inscription below reads:

"To honor a young girl who followed her heart and dreamed a dream in the hope that people everywhere will choose to live in harmony and peace."

I am so glad the girl's two special friends were also immortalized in stone, there in the park, too. That's right, it's me, Fredrick and Malibu Kool Kat. The statue really belongs to anyone who tries to make the world a better place. I hope it is an inspiration for all who see it.

What a grand year of great adventures it had been for me, Fredrick and Kool Kat – a year full of memories to last a lifetime!

Amazing Adventures of Fredrick the Butterfly With Karen & Malibu Kool Kat are loosely based on some of the Author's True Life experiences! See original Award Winning Book *Fredrick The Butterfly*

"May Peace and Love be With You Always!"
—Karen Smythe

Could there be more adventures to come?

Karen Really Did This!

"Malibu resident takes peace flags across Asia"
Malibu Surfside News, January, 2015

When Malibu resident Karen Smythe took a three-week cruise across Southeast Asia in December 2014, she took with her messages of peace from approximately 30 Juan Cabrillo Elementary School students.

A string of student-created flags representing nations from around the world traveled with Smythe via cruise ship through a number of Southeast Asian nations including Thailand, Malaysia, Brunei, Indonesia, Cambodia, Vietnam and Singapore.

"I couldn't speak anyone's languages," Smythe said, "so the amazing part was that when I approached people with the flag, I put my hand up with the peace

Karen Smythe (middle) poses with locals in Vietnamese rice paddy field.

sign and their eyes lit up and they wanted to take their picture with it."

For Smythe, she said she often felt as if the people she met were welcoming her spirit when they looked at her with the flag.

"No matter where we went, we all connected and we all wanted peace and love," she said. "It was a deeper interaction with people than I've ever had before."

The flags Smythe took with her were 30 of more than 200 created by Juan Cabrillo Elementary School students in Zoe Langley's afterschool program for the United Nations' Peace Day, which was celebrated on Sept. 21.

"We hung up the flags during a whole week when we celebrated peace, but I thought it would be great if we got these flags around the world so the kids can see the message is going out to other countries," Langely said, adding that a set of flags from the year prior made their way to Russia.

But as the earlier set did in Russia, the flags Smythe took with her disappeared with a local inhabitant: A Malaysian rickshaw driver, Smythe surmised, thought she had given him the flags and took off with them.

Referencing the flags that disappeared in Russia, Langely said she now almost expects the flags will take on a life of their own.

"Maybe he's going to hang them up or talk about them, but the main message was it wasn't about a particular religion or country, it was about humanity and sending a message of peace to humanity," she said.

Smythe's imagination lent its own theory: "Maybe they'll wash up onto Malibu some day," she said.